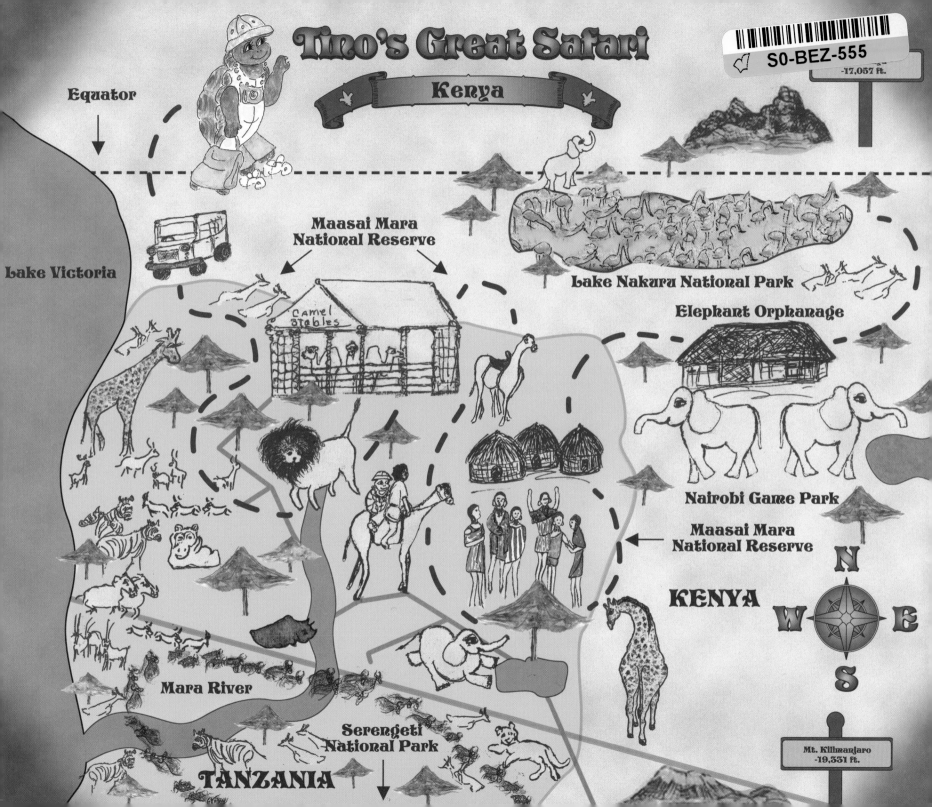

This Book Belongs To:

_____

Tino Turtle Travels
to Kenya
The Great Safari

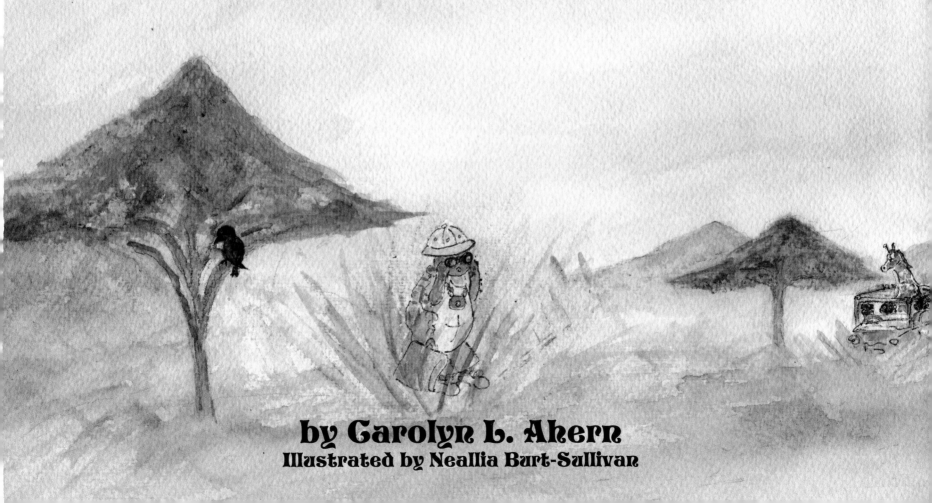

by Carolyn L. Ahern
Illustrated by Neallia Burt-Sullivan

In Memory of Mickey

A beloved friend to the end.

Tino Turtle Travels, LLC
8550 West Charleston Boulevard, Suite 102-398
Las Vegas, Nevada 89117
Copyright © 2009 by Carolyn L. Ahern

info@TinoTurtleTravels.com
www.TinoTurtleTravels.com

The artwork was executed in watercolor, watercolor pencils,
graphite and colored inks on Strathmore cold press paper.
The text was set in 14-point New Century Schoolbook,
and 24-point Storybook.

Written and created by Carolyn L. Ahern.

Printed in China.

CPSIA Tracking Label Information
Production Plant Location: GUANGDONG, CHINA
Production Date: 08/05/2009
Cohort: Batch 1

Library of Congress Control Number: 2007906517

ISBN-13: 978-0-9793158-3-1
ISBN-10: 0-9793158-3-2

TINO TURTLE TRAVELS and the TINO logo
are trademarks of Tino Turtle Travels, LLC.
Registered ® 2006-2009

Once upon a time, there was a desert tortoise named Tino. Tino was a happy turtle in his desert habitat, but he had one wish...he dreamed of traveling to see the world.

One night, in his burrow for his winter sleep, Tino asks his Fairy God Turtle, "Please, Fairy God Turtle...let me travel."

As Tino closes his eyes, his Fairy God Turtle waves her magic wand and grants Tino's wish.

Whoosh! Suddenly, Tino is in *Kenya*…far, far away from his desert burrow.

Tino stretches his neck through the thick brush and sees a big jeep.

A friendly man approaches Tino saying, "You must be Tino Turtle from America."

"Ah…yes," answers Tino. "That's me!"

"We have been expecting you," says the man. "My name is *Jabali*. This is my wife, *Amina*, and our son, *Kito*. We will be your tour guides."

"Let me say *jambo* to you. It means hello in *Swahili*," *Amina* says.

"It's so nice to meet you all," Tino responds. "How do you say how are you?"

"*Hamjambo?*" *Amina* answers.

Tino repeats, "*Hamjambo?*"

"*Hatujambo!* It means we're fine," replies *Jabali*.

"This is Gilda, our baby giraffe," says *Kito*. "She is a special family member."

Tino and Gilda nod their heads to one another.

Jabali directs everyone to the jeep. "We are going on an African *Safari* through the great *Maasai Mara National Reserve*," he says.

"This reserve is famous for the annual migration of the wildebeest and zebras," *Amina* explains.

Kito adds, "It can be risky for them, because hungry predators like lions, cheetahs, and crocodiles are waiting in the grass."

"Whoa!" Tino exclaims. "What if I get trampled by a wildebeest or end up as a crocodile's next meal?"

"Don't worry, Tino," comforts *Amina*. "We will make sure that you are safe."

Tino is thrilled to see giraffes, gazelles, snakes, and elephants, as they rumble through the bush land.

Jabali says, "At the *Maasai Mara*, you will see all kinds of amazing wildlife."

Amina adds, "It's the best place to see the Big Five. The lion, leopard, elephant, buffalo, and rhinoceros…all in one park."

"Oh, and keep an eye out for the Black Manned Lion. If you spot one, be careful! They are dangerous!" *Kito* exclaims.

"Ok," replies Tino. "Thanks for the warning."

During the drive, Tino takes pictures of warthogs, rhinos, zebras, and the many fantastic views of the park.

Jabali tells Tino about one of *Kenya's* well known tribes.

"The *Maasai* have lived in *Kenya* and northern *Tanzania* for centuries and are mighty warriors," *Jabali* explains.

Amina chimes in, "Their clothing is very colorful, with lots of beaded jewelry. Most of them wear *shúkà* wrapped around their bodies."

"What's *shúkà?*" Tino asks.

"The *Maasai's* language is *Maa*. And *shúkà* is *Maa* for sheets," *Amina* replies.

"Are we going to meet the *Maasai* tribe?" Tino asks.

"Yes, and we also hope to see one of their traditional dances," *Amina* replies. "You will be astonished at how high they leap while chanting with their voices."

"Wow! I can't wait," says Tino.

Amina calls out, "Let's stop here, so Tino can take some pictures of the monkeys playing in the tree."

The jeep bounces through grasslands and bush covered hills.

They observe leopards hiding in trees, elephants frolicking in the mud, and the endangered black rhino basking in the sun.

Gilda starts making her funny grunt and snort sounds.

"Can we stop at the river, *tafadhali?*" *Kito* asks. "Gilda is hungry."

"*Ndiyo!*" replies *Jabali*.

Tino asks, "*Kito*, what did you say? *Tafa...?*"

"*Tafadhali* means please and *ndiyo* means yes," *Kito* explains.

"Thank you...I mean, *asante!*" Tino replies.

"Let's have some *chakula*," *Jabali* suggests.

Tino whispers, "What's *chakula?*"

"It's *Swahili* for food," *Kito* replies.

"Mother has prepared *kuku* and *wali* for us,"
Kito says.

"*Kuku* and *wali?*" Tino wonders.

"That's chicken and rice," *Kito* replies.

While *Amina* and *Jabali* set up a small camp by the river, Tino watches Gilda munching on some morsels.

After they finish their meal, *Kito* and Tino
follow Gilda to a nearby Acacia tree.

Gilda picks a few leaves with her long tongue
and shares them with Tino, who savors every
bite.

"These are yummy! Thank you, Gilda," Tino
says.

Then, Tino and Gilda wander off to a nearby
watering hole.

Suddenly, Tino can't believe his eyes! It's the BLACK MANNED LION...jumping out from behind the bushes, heading towards Gilda, ready to attack.

"Look out, Gilda!" Tino shouts.

Tino's heart is pounding with fear. The second the lion goes after Gilda...SNAP...Tino's jaws grab the back of the lion's heel! Then, Tino quickly tucks his head into his shell.

Surprised at his act of courage, Tino sighs with relief as he watches the startled lion run away.

Back at the campsite, the family applauds Tino as their new hero.

Gilda bends her neck down and thanks Tino with a kiss for saving her life.

"Ok, everyone! It's time to continue our *safari*," *Jabali* says.

They arrive at a camel stable where *Jabali* suggests going on a camel excursion.

"What are camels?" Tino inquires.

"Camels are a lot like the burros in your desert," *Kito* says. "They are sure footed on rocky trails and can go a long time without water."

"I see!" Tino replies. "But, what about Gilda?"

"She will walk alongside," *Kito* replies.

The group saddles up the camels and off they go.

They trudge through grazing land, up a rugged trail, to the top of a hill.

Gradually, they become aware of a vibration and pounding of the ground below them. The sound gets louder and louder.

Gilda and the camels get fidgety and anxious. Tino can tell that something is going on.

"It's ok, everyone," *Jabali* assures. "We will be safe up here."

"Look!" *Jabali* exclaims. "There are thousands of gazelles, zebras, and wildebeest…all trying to cross the *Mara River*."

"They migrate in a circle between the *Serengeti Plains* in *Tanzania* and *Kenya's Maasai Mara*. These animals travel 1,800 miles in search of food and water," *Amina* explains.

Jabali adds, "Some make it, some don't. It's a way of life…and a way of survival. This is all a part of the great migration."

Tino is watching the animals thunder by. The spectacle leaves him still and quiet.

Finally, Tino comments, "That is amazing! I just wish that ALL these animals could survive the crossing."

Amina chimes in quickly to cheer up Tino. "Hey, it's time to go to one of my favorite places...*Lake Nakuru National Park*," she says.

"*Ndiyo!* Good idea, let's go!" *Jabali* replies.

After traveling for some time, the group takes a break.

While everyone is enjoying some fresh water and shade from the sun, Tino explores the ground, poking his nose around the shrubs.

Suddenly, Tino's keen sense picks up the cry of an animal in distress. He yells out in panic, "Help! An animal is crying in the bushes... Please hurry!"

The group jumps up to see what Tino has discovered.

"Be careful, Tino!" *Jabali* cautions. "A wounded animal can be unpredictable!"

They all approach together, but Tino is first to see what is on the ground.

"Oh, no…," Tino cries out.

"It's a baby *tembo*," *Jabali* says. "*Tembo* means elephant."

Tino says, "I wonder what happened to her."

He carefully makes contact with the baby and gently rubs his nose against the elephant's trunk, trying to comfort the frightened animal.

As the elephant gets up on her feet, Tino offers some milk. Everyone is glad that she is enjoying it.

Relieved, Tino says, "She seems to feel better already."

Kito pats Tino on his shell and says, "Great job, Tino! This baby might have died if you hadn't found her."

"Can we call her Baby Elle, *tafadhali?*" Tino asks excitedly.

"Sure. That's a great name," *Amina* replies.

"We need to get help for Baby Elle," *Jabali* urges.

"How do we do that?" Tino asks.

"The best place for baby elephants is an elephant orphanage," *Amina* explains. "Baby Elle needs to be in a safe environment, where she will receive medical attention and loving care."

Jabali adds, "There, she will be able to grow up with other elephants and learn the skills needed to survive on her own."

"I see," Tino says. "But I sure will miss her."

Amina asks Tino if he would like to ride on top of Baby Elle.

"She may feel safe with you close to her," *Amina* says.

Jabali helps Tino up, and they move on.

As they come upon a village, they notice the dancing tribal members.

Tino is excited when one of the warriors approaches. *Jabali* tells the chief that they have a special visitor who would like to observe the ceremony.

The warrior is gracious and hands Tino a gift as an act of friendship.

"What a beautiful bead necklace," Tino says. "*Asante*, kind Chief!"

Amina tells Tino that there are many traditional *Maasai* dances for different occasions.

"They are well known for their Jumping Dance," *Kito* says.

Tino is delighted to experience the sights and sounds of the tribe dancing and chanting.

After the ceremony, the chief suggests taking Baby Elle to the elephant orphanage in the *Nairobi Game Park*.

Jabali agrees and thanks the warrior for the hospitality.

The group waves goodbye and leaves for *Nairobi*.

"Tino, once we're near *Nairobi*, we may be able to see *Mt. Kenya* in the distance," *Kito* says. "It's the highest mountain in *Kenya*."

"Really? How high?" Tino asks.

"5,199 meters, which is 17,057 feet," *Kito* responds.

When they finally arrive in *Nairobi*, they make their way to the elephant orphanage where a keeper welcomes the group and immediately attends to Baby Elle.

"So, who is responsible for rescuing this most precious baby?" he asks.

Kito replies, "Tino…Tino saved her!"

"Great job, Tino!" praises the keeper. "And you all did the right thing by bringing her here."

"Let me show you around the orphanage," says the keeper. "I promise that we will take good care of her."

Tino sees some of the elephants enjoying a mud bath and is happy to know that Baby Elle will have new friends to play with.

As the group gets ready to leave, Baby Elle offers her trunk in friendship, and they all say goodbye.

Continuing their camel excursion, *Amina* explains that *Lake Nakuru National Park* is home to over 400 species of birds.

"It has one of the largest gatherings of Pink Flamingos in the world," *Amina* says.

Finally, they reach *Lake Nakuru*. It is glistening with the brilliant pink color of thousands of flamingos.

"Wow! This is awesome!" Tino exclaims.

All of a sudden, Tino is drawn to the shoreline. Only he can hear the voice of his Fairy God Turtle, calling him home.

Realizing this, he turns to his friends and says, "I'm sorry, but it's time for me to go."

"I must return to my burrow! Spring is almost here…my hibernation will soon be over…and my dream will end," Tino explains.

"I wish you could stay longer," *Kito* says. "We have enjoyed your company and hope that we will remain friends forever."

"Likewise," says Tino. "This has been a great *safari*. Thanks for our adventure together. *Kwa heri!*"

"*Kwa heri*, Tino!"

His friends wave farewell as they watch Tino fly away, sitting on top of a majestic Pink Flamingo.

Tino's Fairy God Turtle waves her magic wand, and…

Whoosh! Suddenly, Tino is back home in his desert burrow. His eyes open to the warmth of a spring breeze, the sound of birds singing, and the smell of cactus blossoms.

Tino joyfully says out loud, "Thank you Fairy God Turtle…'til next time we travel… Thank you."

THE END

Tino Turtle Travels to Kenya - The Great Safari - Glossary

Amina	a-*mee*-na	African female name (Meaning: Truthful; Trustworthy)
Asante (sana)	a-*san*-tay (*sa*-na)	Thank you (very much)
Chakula	cha-*koo*-la	Food; Meal
Hamjambo?	ham-*jam*-boh	How are you all?
Hatujambo	ha-too-*jam*-boh	We're fine (used in reply to Hamjambo)
Hujambo?	hoo-*jam*-boh	How are you? (to one person)
Jabali	ja-*ba*-lee	African male name (Meaning: Rock)
Jambo	*jam*-boh	Hello; Hi
Kenya	*kayn*-ya	Country in East Africa (along the Indian Ocean, at the equator)
Kito	*kee*-toh	African male name (Meaning: Jewel; Precious child)
Kuku	*koo*-koo	Chicken
Kwa heri	kwa *hay*-ree	Goodbye; Bye
Lake Nakuru National Park	na-*koo*-roo	Park around Lake Nakuru (central Kenya, south of Nakuru)
Maa	ma	Language of the Maasai tribe
Maasai (Masai)	ma-*sa*-ee	Name of one African tribe in Kenya & northern Tanzania
Maasai Mara National Reserve	ma-*sa*-ee *ma*-ra	Large park reserve in south-western Kenya
Mara River	*ma*-ra	River of Africa, flowing through Kenya and Tanzania
Mt. Kenya	*kayn*-ya	Highest mountain in central Kenya; second highest in Africa
Mt. Kilimanjaro	keel-ee-man-*ja*-roh	Highest mountain in Africa (northeast Tanzania, near Kenya border)
Nairobi	nai-*roh*-bee	Capital and largest city of Kenya; Most populous city in East Africa
Nairobi Game Park	nai-*roh*-bee	National park near the city centre of Nairobi.
Ndiyo	n-*dee*-yoh	Yes
Nakuru	na-*koo*-roo	Maa word for dust or dusty place
Safari	sa-*fa*-ree	Trip; Journey; Tour; Adventure travel
Serengeti	sayr-ayn-*gay*-tee	Maa word for Endless Plains
Serengeti Plains	sayr-ayn-*gay*-tee	Largest national park in north-western Tanzania
Sijambo	see-*jam*-boh	I'm fine (used in reply to Hujambo)
Swahili (Kiswahili)	(kee-) swa-*hee*-lee	African language, mainly spoken in East Africa and Congo
Shúkà	*shoo*-ka	Maa word for sheets, worn wrapped around the body
Tafadhali	ta-fa-*dha*-lee	Please
Tanzania	tan-za-*nee*-a	Country in East Africa
Tembo	*taym*-boh	Elephant
Wali	*wa*-lee	Cooked rice

Tino Turtle Travels
to Kenya

Words and Music by Sue Bella